W9-CTO-314

The Bikini Bottom Bike Race

by Scott Sonneborn
illustrated by Warner McGee

Ready-to-Read

Simon Spotlight/Nickelodeon
New York   London   Toronto   Sydney

A shorter version of this book was published in 2007 by Leapfrog Enterprises, Inc. as *The Tour de Bikini Bottom*.

Based on the TV series *SpongeBob SquarePants*™ created by Stephen Hillenburg as seen on Nickelodeon™

SIMON SPOTLIGHT/NICKELODEON

An imprint of Simon & Schuster Children's Publishing Division

1230 Avenue of the Americas, New York, New York 10020

© 2007, 2011 Viacom International Inc. All rights reserved. NICKELODEON, *SpongeBob SquarePants*, and all related titles, logos, and characters are trademarks of Viacom International Inc. Created by Stephen Hillenburg. All rights reserved, including the right of reproduction in whole or in part in any form. SIMON SPOTLIGHT, READY-TO-READ, and colophon are registered trademarks of Simon & Schuster, Inc. For information about special discounts for bulk purchases, please contact Simon & Schuster Special Sales at 1-866-506-1949 or business@simonandschuster.com.

Manufactured in the United States of America 0711 LAK

4 6 8 10 9 7 5 3

ISBN 978-1-4424-1343-6

A shorter version of this book was published in 2007 by Leapfrog Enterprises, Inc. as *The Tour de Bikini Bottom*.

"Patrick, it is time to go!"
SpongeBob shouted.
"We cannot be late!"

The Bikini Bottom Bike Race
was the biggest race in town.
Squidward was competing.
SpongeBob and Patrick were going
to cheer him on.

It was time for the race to start.
"Good luck, Squidward!"
SpongeBob called out.

"I do not need luck," he answered.
"I ride my bike every day. I would
be shocked if I did not win."
"Ready, set, go!" yelled the starter.
And they were off!

But Squidward was not winning.
In fact he was already last!
"I cannot believe it," said
Squidward sadly. "I have been
training for weeks!"

Squidward pedaled as fast
as he could, trying to catch up.

SpongeBob felt bad.
"Squidward really wants to win,"
he said to Patrick. "We should
help him."

"How?" asked Patrick.

"Well, in order to win he needs energy, right?" SpongeBob said.

"What will give him energy?"

"What if we give him this
Krabby Patty?" Patrick suggested.
"Will that help Squidward win?"
"It just might!" said SpongeBob.

"Too bad," Patrick answered.
"Because I wanted to eat it."
"Sorry, Pat, but Squidward needs it
more than you. We have to get it
to him before it is too late!"

SpongeBob caught up with Squidward.
SpongeBob jumped up and tried
to give Squidward the Krabby Patty.
"What are you doing?" cried
Squidward. "I cannot see where
I am going with that in my face!"

Squidward ran off the road
and hit a rock.
He flew into the air and landed
in Goo Lagoon.

"Look what you did!" Squidward
cried angrily.
Now the other bikers were way ahead.
"There is no way I can win now,"
he whined.

"That did not help Squidward,"
Patrick said to SpongeBob.
"We just have to keep trying,"
SpongeBob answered.

So SpongeBob and Patrick
tried something different.
But it did not work.

Then they tried something else.
That did not work either.

Then they tried a different something else.

But after all they did to help him, Squidward was still in last place! Then Patrick had an idea. "If trying to help Squidward win is making him lose, maybe trying to make him lose will help him win!"

"That's it!" cried SpongeBob.
"I am glad I have a smart friend
like you, Patrick."

SpongeBob and Patrick tried to think of something that would make Squidward lose.

After a few minutes they had it!

There was a sign on the road
telling the bikers which way
to go to reach the finish line.
SpongeBob turned it around
when he saw Squidward coming.

Soon Squidward rode by the sign.
He read it and then pedaled
the wrong way up a steep hill
to the edge of a cliff.

"Yaaarrrggghhh!" yelled Squidward,
  as he flew over the mountain.
"Can you hear what Squidward
  is saying?" asked SpongeBob.
"I think he is trying to thank us!"
  Patrick answered.

The other bikers were almost
at the finish line when Squidward
fell right on top of them!
The race was over.

And Squidward had won by a nose!
"I did it!" cried Squidward.

"We did it!" yelled SpongeBob
and Patrick, cheering.